ONIONS AND GARLIC

AN OLD TALE

Onions and Garlic is a universal tale
that can be found in different versions all over the globe. Eric A.
Kimmel's retelling is derived from one in the *Aggadah*, the collection of stories
gathered from the *Talmud*. Hayyim Nahman Bialik, the first great modern Hebrew
poet, wrote a version of the tale in verse called *The Knight of Onions and the
Knight of Garlic*.
Katya Arnold prepared the artwork using acrylic and watercolor, with a
separate overlay for the black line.

To Rose and Mayer, on
their 50th wedding anniversary
E.A.K.

For Sonia and Boris,
garlic addicts!
K.A.

Library of Congress Cataloging-in-Publication Data
Kimmel, Eric A.
Onions and garlic : an old tale / retold by Eric A. Kimmel;
illustrated by Katya Arnold.
p.   cm.
Summary: The youngest of a merchant's three sons proves that he is
not as foolish as he was thought to be when he trades a sackful of
onions for a fortune in diamonds.
ISBN 0-8234-1222-9 (hardcover : alk. paper)
[1. Jews—Folklore.   2. Folklore.]   I. Arnold, Katya, ill.   II. Title.
PZ8.1.K5670p   1996   95-32707   CIP AC
[398.2]—dc20

ONIONS AND GARLIC

AN OLD TALE

RETOLD BY ERIC A. KIMMEL

PICTURES BY KATYA ARNOLD

HOLIDAY HOUSE
NEW YORK

Once upon a time there lived a merchant
who had three sons: Gedalyah, Hananyah, and Getzel.
Getzel was the youngest. His father and brothers called
him "Getzel-Nahr," which means "Getzel the Fool."
Getzel wasn't stupid, but he was kindhearted and
trusting—unfortunate qualities in a merchant.
Whenever he set out with goods to trade, he tried
too hard to please the people he bargained with.
He ended up selling his goods for less than they cost.
"Getzel, how could you be so foolish!"
his father complained.
"Getzel the Fool has done it again,"
his two older brothers smirked, shaking their heads.

The day came when Getzel's father refused to allow him to trade anymore. He had to stay home, adding up the accounts, while his brothers followed the trade routes over land and sea. Getzel longed to see the world. He pleaded with his father to send him out with a merchant caravan, or find him a place on a sailing ship. His father refused.

"You will never be a trader, Getzel. You believe every sad story you hear. You pay the first price asked. You let others set the value of your merchandise. If I gave you something to trade, you would only be cheated again."

"Then send me out with goods of little value. If I am cheated, you will not lose much. Perhaps I may come home with a profit. You have little to lose and something to gain."

Getzel argued so well that his father changed his mind. He found Getzel a place aboard a merchant ship and gave him some goods to trade, the cheapest he could find—a large sack of onions.

"Thank you, Father," Getzel said. "I will do my best to bring home something of value."

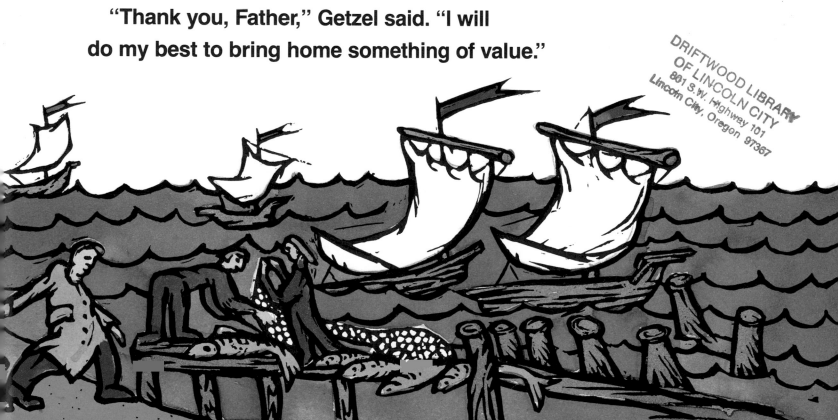

"It will be enough if you bring yourself home safely."

Getzel's father wiped tears from his eyes as the ship set sail.

Of all his sons, he loved Getzel best.

The ship sailed from port to port. Getzel tried his best to sell his onions, but the other merchants only laughed at him. "Farmers, not merchants, sell onions," they scoffed. Nobody wanted to buy them. Getzel had to eat his onions himself to keep from starving.

One night, while the ship was still at sea, a hurricane arose.

Howling winds tore away the sail and blew over the mainmast.

"Our ship is sinking! Swim for your lives!" the captain cried.

A giant wave crashed over the ship, sweeping Getzel and his onions overboard. The anguished cries of his fellow passengers rang in his ears as the ship sank beneath the waves.

The storm passed. One by one the stars came out. Getzel drifted
alone through the night, clinging to his sack of onions.
Morning found him cast up on a deserted beach.
Sparkling pebbles covered the shore as far as Getzel could see.
He picked up a few of the pebbles and discovered they
were diamonds! The smallest was as large as a bean.
Some were as big as goose eggs.
Getzel filled his pockets with the precious stones in case
he should need some money. Then he shouldered his sack of onions
and went in search of food, water,
and human beings.

Before long he came to a city. Getzel discovered that its people spoke a language similar to his own. He asked where he could find something to eat. They directed him to a cookshop.

"I would like to order a meal," Getzel told the cook.

"How will you pay for it?" the cook asked. And no wonder! Getzel's hair was stiff with brine and his clothes were all in rags.

"With these!"

Getzel took a handful of diamonds from his pocket. The cook sneered. "Diamonds aren't worth anything. They are so common that we don't bother picking them up."

Discouraged, Getzel turned away. The cook took pity on him. "I won't refuse a hungry stranger. Come inside. You may have as much soup as you can hold."

Getzel followed the cook into the kitchen.
The cook ladled out a bowl of soup. Getzel began to eat.
The soup had a savory flavor, but something seemed
to be missing. Getzel realized what it was.

"This is fine soup, but it would taste even better if you added some onions," Getzel said.

The cook stared at him in surprise. "What are onions?"

"Don't you grow onions in your country?" asked Getzel.

"I never heard of them."

"I will show you one." Getzel took an onion from his sack. He peeled off the skin and cut a little piece for the cook to taste.

"This is wonderful!" the cook exclaimed. "What do you do with onions?"

"You can do everything with them," Getzel said. "They can be cooked, fried, grilled. They are good with soup, meat, bread, salads . . ."

"Show me," the cook said.

Getzel chopped some onions and added them to the soup. He fried onions in a skillet. He added them to a salad. Then he served the onion meal to the cook.

"We must show this to the king," the cook exclaimed.
He and Getzel went at once to the royal palace.
The cook told the king about the amazing new vegetable.
"I would like to taste one of these onions," the king said.
Getzel peeled an onion for the king.
"Extraordinary!" the king cried, taking a bite of onion.
He said to Getzel, "You must show my chefs
how to cook with onions."
He sent Getzel to the royal kitchens, where Getzel helped
the chefs prepare an onion dinner for the king.
"I never knew food could taste so good,"
the king declared.

"How many onions do you have?" asked the king.

"Nearly a sackful," Getzel replied. "They are easy to grow.
I will show you how to plant them. Then you can have as many as you like."

"I will buy all the onions in your sack. What do you want for them?"
asked the king.

"Not much. A sack of diamonds from your beach will be enough."

"Is that all?" the king said. "I can do better than that.

I will give you a hundred sacks of diamonds, and a ship

to carry you back to your country."

So Getzel the Fool made a good bargain at last.

When Getzel returned home with a hundred sacks of diamonds, his father and brothers could not believe their eyes. Nor could they believe their ears when Getzel told them about his adventures.

"Imagine that! A land where onions are worth more than diamonds," Gedalyah said.

Hananyah replied, "If the king would give that much for onions, imagine what he would pay for garlic!"

The two brothers purchased enough garlic to fill a small ship.
Then they set sail for Getzel's island. They arrived after a long voyage.

Gedalyah and Hananyah looked around with astonishment.
Everything Getzel had told them was true. They walked along
the beach, picking up diamonds as big as goose eggs.

"Our fortune is made!" Gedalyah said.

He and Hananyah set out for
the royal palace. They found
it standing in the middle of
a vast field of onions.

Gedalyah and Hananyah came before the king.
Each carried a large sack of garlic. Bowing low, they said,
"Your Majesty, we are merchants from a distant land.
News has reached us that you love onions."
"Ah, yes!" said the king. "Onions
are wonderful. I eat them all the time. I do
not know how I ever lived without onions."
"Then you will be pleased to hear that we have brought
you something better than onions," Hananyah said.
"What could be better than onions?" the king asked.
"Garlic," Gedalyah answered.
"Garlic? What is garlic?"
"We will show you."

The two brothers took their
sacks of garlic to the royal kitchens.
They showed the king and the royal chefs
how to add garlic to soups, stews, sauces,
and salads. They demonstrated how it could be roasted and
eaten by itself. The king tasted a piece. He swooned with pleasure.

"You spoke the truth. Garlic is better than onions. How much do you have? I will buy it all."

"We brought a whole shipload," Gedalyah said.

"What do you want in exchange?" asked the king.

"A hundred sacks of diamonds from your beach would be enough," Hananyah told him.

"Diamonds!" the king sneered.
"Diamonds aren't worth anything.
Garlic is a delicacy of rare value.
You deserve something worthy of that gift.
I will give you the most precious
treasure in my kingdom."
"What could be more precious than diamonds?"
Gedalyah and Hananyah wondered.
The king said, "You will see."

Gedalyah and Hananyah returned home after a voyage
of many months. Their father met them at the harbor.

"Did you find Getzel's island?"

he asked as he came aboard their ship.

"We did."

"Was the king pleased to learn about garlic?"

"He was."

"And did you trade the garlic for diamonds?"

"Not exactly, Father," Gedalyah sighed.

"The king didn't think diamonds were valuable enough."

"What did he give you instead?

Rubies?   Emeralds?   Pearls?"

Gedalyah and Hananyah raised the hatch
so their father could see for himself.
He peered down into the hold
and found
it filled
with . . .

Onions!